tale of
A TAIL

Margaret Mahy
illustrated by Tony Ross

Orion
Children's Books

First published in Great Britain in 2014
by Orion Children's Books
This paperback edition was first published in Great Britain in 2015
by Orion Children's Books
an imprint of Hachette Children's Group
Published by Hodder & Stoughton
Orion House
5 Upper St Martin's Lane
London WC2H 9EA
An Hachette UK Company

1 3 5 7 9 10 8 6 4 2

A catalogue record for this book is available from the British Library.

ISBN 978 1 4440 1084 8

Printed and bound in Great Britain by Clays Ltd, St Ives plc

The paper and board used in this paperback are natural and recyclable
products made from wood grown in sustainable forests. The
manufacturing processes conform to the environmental regulations
of the country of origin.

www.orionbooks.co.uk

tale of
A TAIL

Also by Margaret Mahy

Wonderful Me!

Wait for Me!

Watch Me!

The Great Piratical Rumbustification

For Younger Readers

A Lion In The Meadow

The Man Whose Mother Was a Pirate

Chocolate Porridge

The Witch Dog

The Boy Who Made Things Up

There's a King in the Cupboard

· Contents ·

Two Toms in Prodigy Street

It was Sunday.

Three days earlier, on Thursday, Tom and his mum had moved into Number One, Prodigy Street, a short street on the very edge of town.

'Why is our street called Prodigy Street?' he asked his mum. 'What does "Prodigy" mean? Does it mean that the people who live in this street get *prodded*?'

'A prodigy is a wonder, a magical surprise,' his mum told him.

'I can't see why our street has that name,' said Tom. 'It's just an ordinary street, like all the other streets in town.'

'Oh come on! We don't really know much about it yet,' Tom's mum said. 'I mean, we do know it's a lot closer to your school than the street we left behind us. You won't have to catch a bus anymore. But when it comes to magical surprises – well, we haven't lived here long enough to be sure. Who knows? This street may have a few shocks waiting for us. Go out to the gate. Look up and down and see if you can see anything prodigious coming our way. And if you do see anything remarkable, come in straight away and tell me all about it.'

'I won't be able to see anything,' mumbled Tom. 'I've got eyes, but I'm not the sort of kid who sees things – well, not magical ones.'

'Go out and practice looking,' his mum told him. 'We don't know what might be lurking out in there in Prodigy Street.'

2

Tom sighed.

'Go!' commanded his mum. 'Look right! And then look left! You just never know!'

So Tom went out to the gate and looked first right, and then left, exactly as he had been told to.

It was a winter afternoon, cloudy and cool, and the breeze blowing down Prodigy Street made him shiver. The trees that grew on either side of

the street shivered too, stretching bare branches towards the clouds, rather as if they knew there was blue sky somewhere behind them, and they must scratch those clouds apart to get at it. But, although the trees were bare, Tom suddenly felt it was almost as if he and his mum had moved into a forest, and Prodigy Street was a secret road winding through that forest, leading them on and on, then on again. From somewhere further down the street he could hear a strange sound . . . a mysterious yowling. It made the street seem more like a forest than ever. He could see houses, of course, houses that looked ordinary enough with their lawns, gardens, neat hedges and cats sitting on letter boxes. Perhaps it was one of those cats that was yowling so furiously – so very furiously that Tom took a step backward. And, as he did so, he saw, there – at the end of the street – one particular red roof, the roof of a very big house, rising above all the other roofs and even above the trees too. It seemed to be looking back at him out of its own top window. The wind blew, the trees waved, and the top window in that red-roofed house suddenly seemed to be winking at him.

Then Tom noticed there was a big van at the gate of that house, a furniture van, perhaps the very same van that had brought their own furniture to their own new house only two days before. It seemed, all at once, that someone else must be moving into Prodigy Street for the first time. Tom slid out of the gate and then along the footpath so he could get some idea of just who might be moving in. It might be someone of his own age . . . someone who could be a friend to him.

Yes! It certainly was a strange, old house. You could tell it had once stood alone, surrounded by wild meadows and grazing horses, but slowly, slowly the town must have crept out towards it, street by street, shop by shop, house by house, and closed in around it, taking it prisoner. Yet, even though it now had those other houses crowding in on it, even though it was at the very top of a town street called Prodigy Street, in a way it still seemed a lonely house . . . a house that had closed its doors tightly, and let old plum trees grow up over its windows, after shutting in on itself behind a tall gate with spikes of iron along its top. Tom went back inside to tell his mum what he had seen.

'We've been here since Thursday,' he said. 'Those people moving into that old house with the spiky gate are the true Prodigy Street strangers.'

'Twenty-two Prodigy Street,' said Tom's mum, as if she knew all about it. 'I think that house is a bit too tumble-down for anyone to want to live there for long. Someday someone will pull it all down and build a block of flats there. Flats with tiny gardens out at the back, perhaps. Of course they'll have to clear all the weeds away first, probably cut down all those old plum trees too.'

Tom went back to his new front gate. He couldn't help feeling very curious about that house when he saw the big furniture vans moving in . . . just who was going to live there? Though Prodigy Street had those tall trees growing on either side of it, though smart cars went sliding out of it in the morning and back again in the evening, as far as he could tell he was the only boy living there. He was half-friendly with a girl called Sarah, three houses along (they were in the same class at school), but it would be great to have a boy-neighbour too, someone he could play with after school. Mind you, every now and then (or so he had been told), the Cat-Kickers, a gang of boys from three streets over, all from Ominous Avenue, would burst into Prodigy Street to trample on the edges of gardens and kick any cats they could find. But those boys were all a lot older than Tom, and anyway he didn't want to have anything to do with cat-kicking. After all, he and his mum had an old pet

7

cat called Sox, and he certainly did not want Sox
to be kicked around. So he hoped whoever it was
who was moving into that house with the jungle
garden would not be a Cat-Kicker, and would
leave Sox alone if Sox ever went wandering out
along Prodigy Street.

'The man who's moved in at the end of the
street,' his mum said at dinner that night. 'A bit
of a strange guy, I'm told. Well, he'd need to be,
to move into a house that is almost falling to
pieces.'

'Perhaps he's brought some good glue with
him,' said Tom.

'He'll need it,' said Tom's mum. 'What was

his name? Mr Marvellous, wasn't it? No! I remember now. Mr Mirabilis!'

'Does he have any children?' asked Tom.

'I don't think so,' said his mum. 'He does have a dog, though!'

This was interesting. Tom already knew there were no dogs in Prodigy Street. Somehow it seemed everyone in Prodigy Street had decided a cat would be the easiest sort of pet to live with. Mind you, if that was a cat he had heard yowling a little earlier he might have to be careful. It had been a very savage sound, and cats had pointed teeth as well as sharp claws.

Anyhow, next day, Monday, after he had come home from rugby practice, Tom kept spying on that old house at the end of the street, and at last he saw not a furniture van but an actual car – a graceful, black car (old, but well-polished) – glide up the street and park outside that spiky gate. A moment later

a tall man slid from that car and stood looking around him. He just *had* to be Mr Mirabilis. He somehow matched that name. He was very tall.

His long silver hair blew out round him, and for a moment he looked as if he had a dandelion puff-ball for a head, and instead of wearing a coat to protect himself against that cold, winter wind, he was wearing a long cloak that billowed around him like a black whirlpool. It was lined with glowing red silk, so Mr Mirabilis looked as if he was smuggling a wild sunset into that house on the corner.

Tom opened his own gate and jogged quickly down the footpath on his side of Prodigy Street, until he stood opposite that polished, black car. He hesitated for just a moment. Then he crossed the road.

'Hi!' he called. 'Are you moving in?'

The man barked at him . . . at least Tom *thought* the man barked at him . . . but then he saw that the man was not alone. He had a small dog beside him, a small, shaggy dog with pointed ears, little wizard's houses filled with shadows, a black nose and a ginger-brown moustache. There

11

was a parting that ran from the tip of his nose to the end of his stubby tail, and when the dog saw Tom it wagged that tail as if it was writing a secret message in the air behind it.

'We're both moving in,' said the man. He pointed down at the dog. '*He* chose this house. He likes the thought of living in a jungle. So, you're one of my new neighbours, are you? What's your name?'

'Tom!' said Tom. 'It's short for Thomas!' he added.

The man's mouth fell open as if in surprise.

'That's remarkable,' he said. 'That's my name too. How do you spell yours?'

Tom spelt his name in full.

'Well, that's a little differently from the way I spell mine,' said the man. 'My name begins with a "T" of course, but it ends with a "Z" – TOMASZ. My name is Polish. Still, it shows how names travel around the world, leaping from one country to another. Two Toms, one Thomas and one Tomasz, both moving into Prodigy Street from different directions, and living at different ends of it. What do you think of that?' he asked his dog.

The dog jumped up at Tom, signalling with its shaggy paws. His mouth was just a little bit open . . . he seemed to be smiling under his moustache.

'Oh! That's unusual,' said the man. 'He's usually rather haughty with strangers. Perhaps he's being friendly because we share the same name.'

'What's your dog called?' asked Tom. 'Is he called Tomasz too?'

'Oh no! But *his* name is rather remarkable,' said the new neighbour. 'His name is spelt N-a-j-k-i . . . but, when you say it properly, it sounds like Naykee. Polish as well! We match. Anyhow, he's a clever dog, and he's the one who helped me look for a house. And he thought this one would be just the place for us. Do you think we'll enjoy living in this street?'

'I think it's a bit too ordinary,' said Tom. 'I'd like it to be a bit . . . a bit sort of *wilder*! Not dangerous or anything! Just a bit more adventurous. Mind you, I heard something yowling very fiercely when I was looking around before.'

'Well, things often quieten down during the winter,' said the new neighbour. 'Perhaps it will grow more exciting in spring and summer.'

'It would be great if it was spring now,' said Tom. 'I wish the trees were flowering.' And Najki barked as if he was agreeing with Tom, switching his stubby tail up and down.

Then an astonishing thing happened.

There was that cold breeze blowing down Prodigy Street, but it wasn't like a true wind – it wasn't strong enough to shake those big plum trees. Nevertheless suddenly all the branches over the fence quivered, as if they had had a sudden fright or had caught a glimpse of someone they recognised. Then, while Tom stared up at them,

wondering just what was going on, every single plum tree in that wild garden exploded into blossom. Delicate white flowers appeared on every twig, all wide open as if they were drinking in the day around them, all nodding at Tom as if they knew him. Najki barked again, possibly just as astonished as Tom, who stood gazing up into those spring-time trees, all flowering in winter.

And suddenly he remembered his new neighbour was called Mr Mirabilis . . . a magical name. Tom stared over at him, his mouth hanging open just a little.

'There's nothing wrong with wishing trees would flower,' said Mr Mirabilis. 'That's a perfectly reasonable wish. But sometimes you have to be careful what you wish for. Make sure you remember that, now my dog and I have come to live in Prodigy Street. If you have to wish for anything, do wish very carefully indeed.'

Tom looked up once more into those blossoming trees.

'I'd better go home,' he said at last. 'My mum might be wondering where I've got to.'

But that was just an excuse. He wasn't exactly scared by what he had just seen, but it was as if he had too much to think about. How could winter trees leap into full blossom, and how could those blossoming plum trees look so beautiful and yet be a little frightening at the same time? He ran home as fast as he was able.

Later he came out to his gate again, and looked carefully towards that old house with the shining car parked outside it, feeling that merely looking at it might cause something remarkable to happen. There was no sign of Mr Mirabilis or Najki, but Tom could see that those plum trees were still blossoming. From the distance it almost looked as if snow had fallen all around that red roof.

Tom went back inside to hide in his bedroom. He had lived in Number One, Prodigy Street for three whole days, but suddenly, just as he thought he was getting used to it, the street had become a different place . . . not just a new place, but a truly mysterious one. That distant yowling to begin with . . . and then the plum trees. There was no way he could work out just how all this was happening.

· 2 ·

Barking On!

A new house is a new house, whether you are a person or a dog. I could tell as soon as I arrived in Prodigy Street there would be plenty of cats for me to chase. Prodigy Street seemed to be a street that had a cat for every house. But there were a lot of things about Prodigy Street I still needed to find out, plenty of places I would need to explore. Inside my new house

things were taking shape. My dog baskets were
set out, waiting for me just in case I felt tired.
My blue rug was there, ready for me to cuddle
into. But I didn't want to cuddle into anything
until I had explored my new place. I liked the
street, and yet I felt there was something . . .
well, something dangerous lurking about out
there, so I wanted to get out and about a bit
. . . to smell gateposts and telegraph poles . . .
check things over. I could tell at a glance that
my pet, Tomasz, would be busy for a while, so I
would need to find some other pet I could take
for a walk or two, just to do my own sort of
adventuring, just to check up on that occasional
yowling, just to find what heroes and villains
might be living in Prodigy Street. The boy
seemed promising. After all, his name was Tom,
a name I already enjoyed. It was a good sign.
Mind you, I don't want to take just anyone for
a walk . . . I'd prefer to take my own Tomasz.
But I could tell he would be busy unpacking

and so on over the next day or two. Of course I could have wagged at him, and then he would have to do what I wanted him to do, but I had made up my mind to give him a break.

That night, just before I went to sleep, I tried sending that other, down-the-road Tom a secret command, but I was interrupted.

'Who are you?' I asked, but there was no real reply. Then, suddenly, I did get a picture in my head of someone furry, someone with narrow green eyes and long, white teeth. A cat, I thought. A particularly savage cat! It yowled at me. But of course I did not want my messages interrupted by a mere cat, even if it did happen to be a green-eyed yowler.

'I'll try again early tomorrow morning,' I thought. 'I'll go exploring.' Then I burrowed in under my blankets, cuddled up to my toy, and went to sleep.

21

3

Tigering a Cat

*N*ext day was Tuesday, but it was an unexpected holiday. The inside of the school was being painted, and the painters had arranged to be allowed to paint without a lot of interruptions. Tom woke up absolutely pleased that he did not have to go to school. Yes! The day was already full of sunshine, and for some reason Prodigy Street, waiting quietly just outside the gate, seemed to be full of possible adventures.

Tom made his bed, had a breakfast of toast and

orange juice, and went into that day. Straightaway he caught himself looking down Prodigy Street, spying on that pointed red roof rising from a jungle of weeds and blossoming plum trees. He was half-hoping to see Mr Mirabilis. Was he likely to be tidying the jungle, trying to make his house and garden match all the other houses and gardens in Prodigy Street? Was he the sort of man who would wear a swirling black and scarlet cloak while he was digging out weeds?

However there was no sign of any movement under those strange, blossoming plum trees in that end-of-the-street jungle.

While he was spying on the house with the red roof, someone called his name. It was Sarah from Number Seven, three houses away on his side of the street, the girl who was in his class at school. She came towards him, wearing blue jeans and blue ribbons in her looped-up plaits, half-walking, half-dancing, and pointing at her heels.

'Isn't this weird?' she was shouting. Tom looked at her feet and saw a small black-and-white cat with long white whiskers, rubbing against her right leg. But that cat was not alone. Yesterday's unexpected dog Najki was there too, also rubbing against Sarah's leg – her left one. And the really strange thing was that the cat did not seem in the least bit worried at having a rough-coated, pointy-eared, stubby-tailed dog alongside him.

Tom set off to join Sarah.

'Isn't it weird?' she said again. 'That's my cat Mouser down there, and mostly Mouser hates dogs. They make him fluff up and hiss. But this dog came to meet us, and now they seem quite friendly.'

'Is Mouser a yowler?' asked Tom.

'He can mew,' said Sarah, looking puzzled for a moment. 'Oh, I know who you're thinking of. There's a real yowler in that house over there . . . in Number Five.' She pointed behind her along Prodigy Street, at a house with a high holly hedge and a black gate with a padlock on it. 'They keep that cat shut in because he is so ferocious. He does purr sometimes and then he sounds like a speeding motor-mower. But *my* cat Mouser is soft and friendly. Look at him! Hey! Maybe Mouser thinks this dog is a sort of dog-cat. Or maybe this dog thinks Mouser is a sort of cat-dog. I've never seen a dog in Prodigy Street before. Where do you think he comes from?'

'He moved into that old house yesterday,' said Tom, pointing to the red roof at the end of Prodigy Street. 'I suppose he's out having a look around, and getting *used* to us all.'

'Maybe he wants a bit of a walk,' said Sarah. 'Let's just set off and see if he follows.'

But when they set off Najki did not follow them. He ran on ahead, sniffing at gateposts as he went, while (and this was the astonishing thing) Mouser padded along after him. It was as if that cat knew they were going to have fun somehow, and he did not want to be left out of it.

'Weird!' said Sarah yet again. 'I mean, taking a cat for a walk as well as a dog. Mouser's never come along with me like this before. And that dog seems to be choosing the way for us. Let's go after him.'

They were coming towards a small corner in Prodigy Street. A narrow little alley called Wonder Walk ran off to the right – a walk that was shaded, even on a bright day, by hedges and trees, which made it seem a little spooky. It was usually a quiet alley, almost invisible, but today, as they passed it, there was a sudden yelling and then a cry of triumph. Six big, wild boys, all older than Tom and Sarah, burst into Prodigy Street, and, though they had never seen all those boys before, Tom and Sarah knew just who they must be.

'The Cat-Kickers!' Sarah cried. 'It's the Cat-Kickers!'

And indeed it was that villainous Cat-Kicker gang, racing into Prodigy Street along Wonder Walk from Ominous Avenue. And, before Sarah or Tom could do anything about anything, that gang had leaped at them, pushed them over and snatched up Mouser.

'Catch that cat!' they yelled to one another, laughing aloud. 'Kick that cat to Kingdom Come!'

'Leave my cat alone!' screamed Sarah, picking herself up and charging at them, but they took no notice of her. Instead one of them actually began swinging Mouser around by his tail, while the others pointed and laughed.

'We're the Cat-Kickers!' they cried callously. Mouser tried to twist himself around and climb up his own tail, hoping to scratch the boy who was whirling him, but the Cat-Kicker who had hold of his tail was swinging him around much too wildly.

'Save Mouser!' Sarah screamed again, but one of the gang pushed her over for the second time. 'Help me!' she called, rolling on the footpath. 'Save Mouser!'

'I'll have a go,' Tom mumbled, charging at the gang too, even though there were six of them, and every one of them big enough to boot him up and away. He would do his best, but, even as he charged at them, he was sure his best would not be good enough. Mouser was screaming a great cat scream (almost, but not quite, a yowl). He was being swung backwards and forwards, then around and around.

'Swing the cat and squash the cat!' yelled the gang triumphantly, just as one of the gang sent Tom flying backwards over a low wall and into the daisy bushes of a Prodigy Street garden. Najki leaped over the little wall too, and pushed his wet, black nose against Tom's nose. Peering at the dog through daisy bushes, Tom saw Najki was wagging his tail up and down.

'He must think this is some sort of game,' thought Tom wildly.

'Swing the cat and swoop the cat!' the Cat-Kicker gangsters were shouting out in the street beyond.

'Save Mouser,' Tom said aloud, though he didn't know quite who he was saying it to. 'I wish we could save Mouser. I wish something bigger and stronger would come roaring in and help us.' Najki wagged his tail even harder. It was strange to see him wagging it up and down. Most dogs wag sideways.

But then something truly remarkable happened.

Mouser changed. One moment he was a small, black-and-white cat being swung around by his tail, the next he was swelling out as if he was a cat-balloon, changing colour as he

swelled. And instead of screaming cat-screams, he was snarling and roaring. He grew big . . . bigger . . . even bigger . . . much too big for any Cat-Kicker to swing – too big, even, for a Cat-Kicker to hold. Too big for *anyone* to hold! The boy dropped Mouser, who sprang away from him. Sarah and Tom gasped with astonishment. Mouser was turning into a tiger . . . not just any old tiger but a super-tiger! Now he had been set free, he swept around on the gang, letting out

a great super-tiger roar, and then he sprang at them – front paws up, claws out! Such tiger teeth as well! And such a powerful spring! All six Cat-Kicker bullies were instantly terrified. Their shouting and jeering turned into screams of fear, as they swung around wildly, and raced back into the shadows of Wonder Walk with that totally unexpected tiger bounding after them, roaring and raking the air with claws like curved daggers.

Tom picked himself up and stood still, staying just where he was. After all, he was terrified, and he could see Sarah was scared out of her wits as well. Having your pet cat suddenly turn into a tiger certainly gives you something to think about.

'What's happening?' Sarah was crying. 'Where's my Mouser?'

She darted towards Wonder Walk, but Tom grabbed her arm and pulled her back.

'Don't go there! It might be too dangerous!' he

yelled. In the distance they could hear the gang still screaming with terror, as they raced away down Wonder Walk back to Ominous Avenue.

'What happened?' asked Sarah again, utterly bewildered.

'Mouser turned into a tiger,' replied Tom blankly.

'I know, but he's never done that before,' Sarah said. 'Something *changed* him.'

The voices that had been echoing down Wonder Walk grew silent.

'Has that tiger eaten them all?' Sarah asked – just what Tom was wondering.

'I don't think so,' he said, even though he was not sure. 'I think that the tiger's just . . . just chasing them back home and . . .' (He crossed his fingers as he was saying this. After all, even though the gang were such bullies, he didn't quite want them to be eaten by an accidental wish-tiger.) Then, looking around him in a bewildered way, he suddenly saw Najki, staring down the shadowy Wonder Walk, bobbing his tail up and down as if he was really interested in what had just happened. He certainly did not look as if tigers worried him in the slightest.

'Miaow!' said a voice somewhere in the shadows of Wonder Walk.

'Listen!' cried Sarah. 'A cat. That just has to be a cat. Tigers don't mew, do they?'

'Miaow!' said the voice again, sounding a little louder this time, and that black-and-white Mouser himself came wandering back into Prodigy Street. Tom thought the cat was looking very pleased with himself. His whiskers certainly had a triumphant tilt to them. Sarah sprang forward.

'Mouser! Oh my very best Mouser!' she cried. 'I thought you'd turned into a tiger forever.'

Najki barked.

'Mouser *was* the tiger,' said Tom again, but he only mumbled it. It was so hard to believe that he thought it was best to think it over for a while.

'What's going on?' he was asking himself inside his head. 'Was Mr Mirabilis watching us from some high-up window in that strange, old house, and working a magic spell?'

He looked rather sternly at Najki – the one who just might know what was going on, but Najki immediately looked the other way. If he *did* understand, he wasn't telling anybody. It was Sarah who spoke out.

'It was the *dog*,' she cried. 'I saw him. He wagged his tail in a funny way, and Mouser began to change.'

'Dogs aren't magicians,' said Tom.

'I *saw* him!' Sarah repeated. 'He switched

on his tail like a little electric wand and *tigered* Mouser.' She bent over Najki, patting him and fussing over him. Najki looked pleased.

'Maybe,' Tom agreed, looking at that red pointed roof, rising over the plum blossom. Once again the top window seemed to be winking at him. 'I wish I knew for sure.'

But then, suddenly, he *was* sure. He didn't know the how or why of it all, but inside his head he was utterly certain Sarah was right.

Why was he suddenly so certain? Only a moment before he had been confused by what had happened. Now he was convinced Najki's tail-wagging had somehow transformed a tabby cat into a tiger. Najki had switched his tail up and down and his tail had acted like a magician's wand. Tom was taken aback at being so suddenly sure of this. He thought he would try out some other possibility.

'Maybe it's living in Prodigy Street,' he said to Sarah. 'Prodigy means "wonders".'

'It's the dog,' Sarah said, as if she was absolutely certain she was right. 'There's no doubt about it. Wake up, Tom! That dog's not just a dog . . . he must be a magician as well.'

· 4 ·

More Magical Barking

*W*ell, there you are. That girl knew me almost
at once. She wasn't called Tomasz, or even Tom,
but she was quick off the mark. I was certainly
pleased when she patted me. Mind you, I can
be choosy about being patted. I'm not one of
those dogs that rolls over for everyone. But that
girl, Sarah, she recognised something about
me, and it's great being recognised in the right

40

way by the right people. Somewhere along the
line, when Sarah wishes for something (and
sooner or later everyone always has something
they wish for), I'll grant her that wish – just
see if I don't. Mind you, I hope she doesn't
wish for anything too complicated. Granting
complicated wishes can sometimes make life a
bit too adventurous for the people around you.
Of course, they do get the fun of it all. And me?
Well, it's mostly me who gets the blame. But
oh, what a tail I've got! OK, it's short – but it's
a truly useful tail! There's no doubt about that.
And of course (as I have to keep reminding
you) I'm not just a dog. You could say I'm a
dog and a half.

Beating the Weasels

'Mum,' said Tom after school on Wednesday. 'That man in the house with the big red roof – that man is a *magician* . . .'

'Well he might be, I suppose,' said Tom's mum. 'All those plum trees around his house have blossomed early. But just because he has a name like Mirabilis doesn't mean he is actually magical. And some trees just do come out earlier than others. Some trees even begin to blossom in the late winter.'

'. . . and his dog's a magician too,' Tom went on. 'Yesterday when we were being bullied by the Cat-Kicker gang . . .'

But he could tell his mum wasn't really listening. She was rushing around, tidying the house in the way mums often feel they have to. And, standing there in the afternoon sunlight, Tom found it quite hard to believe that the strange things which had happened yesterday really *had* happened. He wondered about this over and over again as he went out into the garden.

'Sarah's Mouser did turn into a tiger . . . just for a few minutes,' he said aloud, but all around him was yesterday's garden, looking utterly ordinary in its own untidy way. This morning it was hard to believe yesterday's tiger had been real. After all, Tom knew how often he liked to imagine things. He might have *invented* yesterday's strange happenings, and then tricked himself into thinking they were true. But then again, he might actually be able to take a magical dog for walks and, while he was walking that dog, his dream wishes might somehow be made real. Tom felt himself swelling with excitement and pride.

'It's not just the dog,' he thought. 'It's me too. He can grant wishes. OK! But me – I'm the one who knows what to wish for. That dog *needs* me.'

Still guessing about Najki, Tom strolled to and fro restlessly. On the one hand, he liked working it all out for himself. On the other, he felt he should consult an expert, and there was only one expert he could think of. At first he felt rather shy, perhaps even a little scared, at the thought of calling in on Mr Mirabilis, but at the same time he felt he just had to know if there really was something magical springing to life in Prodigy Street . . . if that man in his wild storm-cloud of a cloak (along with his unexpected dog) had secret powers. There was only one way to find out.

So off he set down Prodigy Street once more, pretending to himself he didn't know just where he was going, even though he kept staring at that red roof at the end of the street – that red roof pointing up above the storm of spring plum blossom and winking at him with its upstairs window.

The spiked gate, twice as tall as Tom, was just a little bit open and he slipped through the gap, walking up the drive under that arch of blossom.

Tiny petals fell on him as he walked in. It seemed like a sort of welcome.

And, at last, he came to three stone steps, climbed onto the verandah of the house and stood there, looking at the door – a door of reddish brown wood carved around with faces – smiling faces, frowning faces, laughing faces and weeping faces. In the middle of that door was a huge, bronze knocker, and hanging beside the door was a bronze bell with a golden cord dangling down from it. Tom took a deep breath and knocked three times. Then he pulled on the golden cord, and the bell gave a single, slow chime, filling the verandah around him with mysterious echoes.

Inside the house someone began barking. Then Tom heard footsteps, heavy, soft footsteps coming towards the door. For a moment he wondered if those steps were made by big paws. For a moment he wondered if yesterday's tiger was going to open the door and leap out at him. But when the door did open it was simply opened by Mr Mirabilis with Najki at his feet. Najki had a toy in his mouth, a pink puppet dog, but at the sight of Tom he dropped it, and barked three times.

'Hello! It's that other Tom!' said Mr Mirabilis. 'What can I do for you?'

'I wondered if you'd let me take Najki for a walk,' Tom said. 'I like taking dogs for walks, and I don't have a dog of my own.'

'That's very kind of you,' said Mr Mirabilis. 'I'm still busy unpacking stuff, and I think Najki's a bit tired of being inside. Besides he loves a walk on a sunny morning – a walk with the right people, that is, and you might be just right for him. I'll get you a good lead, though. You won't want him running out in front of cars. It could be dangerous. After all, people do need their cars, don't they? Terrible if your car suddenly turned into a horse trough.'

Najki's lead was plaited out of gold and silver threads. Tom had never seen a lead like it before. Mr Mirabilis attached that lead to Najki's collar and then passed it over to Tom.

'I'll look after him,' Tom promised.

'And he'll look after you,' Mr Mirabilis promised back. 'Just have a good time. Oh, and be very careful what you wish for when Najki's around. The wrong wish can be very dangerous.'

It seemed like strange advice, but perhaps not quite as strange as it would have seemed yesterday.

Tom tried to lead Najki back down the drive, but the dog seemed rather unwilling to go.

'I forgot for the moment,' said Mr Mirabilis. 'He doesn't much like to go out without me. Go on, you silly dog! This is Thomas – another Thomas – and he'll bring you home before too long.'

Najki seemed to understand what Mr Mirabilis said. Suddenly he stopped pulling away from Tom, and they set off together, under those blossoming plum trees. And then, suddenly, Najki became eager to run on ahead out into Prodigy Street. He seemed to know just which way he wanted to go. Tom found himself jogging after the dog as if Najki was in charge.

'He's taking *me* for a run,' Tom thought.

They came out into Prodigy Street, and there, only a few houses in front of them, was Sarah.

'Hi!' she cried as they came towards her. 'I'm going to watch the after-school rugby. Do you want to come too?'

Tom thought this was a good idea, though he did not know if a dog like Najki would enjoy rugby.

'Who's playing?' he asked.

'Our school!' said Sarah, 'and they're playing the team from Weasel.'

(Weasel was the town over the hill. Over the years their school had played many matches against the Weasel School, and the Weasel School had always won. It was a big school, and its rugby team was rough and tough and did not always play fairly. Its players had invented a lot of secret, cheating tricks which Tom and Sarah's school, the Farfetched School, had never quite learned to expect. And every year the tricks were a little bit different from what they had been the year before.)

'I'll cheer loudly,' Sarah said. 'That will encourage our guys.'

Tom made up his mind to cheer loudly too.

As they walked down Prodigy Street, Najki suddenly turned sideways into Wonder Walk. It was as if he already knew where they wanted to go and was taking a shortcut to the school. They followed him, ran quickly across Ominous Avenue and into Farfetched Road. Suddenly the school was there in front of them, and stretched out in front of the school was its sports ground, crowded with people who had come to watch the after-school rugby game. Sarah, Tom and Najki (on that golden lead) were at the back of the crowd to begin with, but they managed to wriggle through until they had a good view of the whole field. Two teams faced one another, waiting for the whistle to blow.

'Just in time,' Tom said. 'Oh dear! Look at that Weasel team. They look way older than our lot. Tougher too!'

'They always look like that,' said Sarah

The Weasel team was certainly a taller and broader team, and every player was scowling over at the Farfetched players as if they were longing to smash them all down, then grind them into the dirt. It was hard to believe Farfetched stood a chance. All the same it seemed Najki was anxious to see the game, no matter who was likely to win. He sat up, looking alert and interested, his pointed ears cocked at a thoughtful angle.

Out in the field a whistle blew and the game began.

Rugby is a muscley-tussley game. You've got to *kick* the ball of course, but sometimes you have to *run* with it, holding the ball under one arm while you push the enemy away with the other. There are front lines and back lines and scrambly scrums which look as if two teams of mad crabs from Mars are struggling against one another.

Of course Sarah and Tom cheered for the Farfetched team, but the Weasel boys were bigger and faster, and when they kicked they never missed. Soon they were leading 15–nil, and anyone could tell the Farfetched boys were not only smaller, but were losing heart. Then one boy, a Farfetched boy, was knocked over and did not get up again.

'He's just pretending,' cried Sarah. 'I could do better than he's been doing, and I could run faster. I wish I was out there being part of the team.'

For some reason, after hearing her say this, Tom looked down at Najki, who began wagging his stumpy tail up and down rather quickly, almost fiercely, Tom thought. And when he looked up again, Tom found that Sarah had disappeared.

A moment ago she had been standing there beside him, and now she had totally vanished. Where could she be? He stared to the left and then to the right. No sign of her. But suddenly the crowd around him began a rowdy, riotous cheering, and when he looked onto the field, anxious to know what was going on, he saw that one Farfetched player had the ball and was streaking along, dodging the Weasel boys, and making a triumphant run to score. But that was not all he saw. This particular speedy player was the only player on the field whose hair was tied back with pink ribbons. Sarah! It was Sarah! And she had actually scored a try. Tom could hardly believe it. Then, a few minutes later, she converted that try with a tremendous kick. This was even harder to believe. Tom looked sternly at Najki who was wagging his tail very briskly.

'Did *you* do that?' he asked. Najki looked back at him from under his tufty eyebrows, then hung out his tongue, waving it like a pink banner.

Tom was so busy guessing about Najki he almost missed the next bit. Sarah got the ball again and scored a second try. Farfetched was catching up. Suddenly the game had become very exciting.

Just about this time one of the Weasel players, furious because Farfetched was unexpectedly doing so well, secretly thumped one of the smaller

Farfetched boys in a bullying Weasel way. The umpire did not see this, but he helped the poor, thumped player to his feet, looked closely at his bruised knees, shook his head and pointed to the sideline.

Tom took a deep breath.

'I wish *I* was playing,' he said, thinking carefully. 'And I wish I was a terrific player – even if it was only for the next hour or so.'

And suddenly – suddenly! – there he was, actually on the field, in the middle of his Farfetched fellows, wearing a Farfetched jersey and ready to join in the Farfetched game. A whistle blew. Something thumped against Tom's chest. The ball! Someone in his team had thrown the ball at him. He grabbed it tightly, and began to run, feeling the Weasel boys closing in on him. Faster! He must go faster.

'Over here!' called a voice he knew, and, without even bothering to look, he threw the ball to Sarah, who shot off down the field.

Immediately the Weasel team forgot Tom and began to close in on Sarah, but she threw the ball sideways again. Tom caught it so cleverly he could hardly believe it himself, dodged a Weasel player far more cunningly than he had ever dodged anyone before, and then he was diving through the air, right over the line and slamming the ball down firmly. He had scored a try. He had actually scored a try. And, just a little later, he kicked that ball right between the posts, something he had always found it difficult to do.

And that was the beginning of the end. The other players in the Farfetched team brightened up. There was no going back. Some, encouraged by the examples Tom and Sarah were setting, improved their game enormously. They caught up with the Weasels. They passed them by one try. Then a whistle blew. Time was out! Farfetched had won the game.

The team was cheered, but the team did some

cheering too. It cheered itself and it particularly cheered Sarah and Tom.

'I didn't know you could play like that!' the coach (really a very fit teacher) cried in amazement. 'You must have natural talent.'

'It was just a one-off thing,' said Tom. 'I don't think I could play like that two days running.'

'You should have a go,' said the coach. 'Come and find me after school tomorrow and I'll give you a trial.'

'What about me?' asked Sarah.

The coach looked at her and sighed deeply.

'Girls playing rugby . . . I just don't know,' he said. 'I wish I did.' And then, all of a sudden, his expression changed. 'Well, why not?' he cried. 'You were terrific as well. Meet us after school tomorrow and we'll see what happens.'

61

At that moment Tom noticed something. Najki was trotting along after them, dragging his golden lead and vigorously wagging his tail up and down.

He remembered Mr Mirabilis saying that people ought to be careful what they wished for.

'What *happened* back there?' Sarah asked, as they made their way back to Prodigy Street. 'I've played a bit of rugby with my cousins, but I've never been as clever as I was this time.'

'I don't know,' said Tom. 'I was pretty good too, wasn't I? Hey! Maybe it's because we live in Prodigy Street.'

He looked sideways, and found Sarah staring across at him in a very suspicious way.

'I've lived in Prodigy Street for ages,' she said, 'and I've never played like that before. Something *happened* to me.'

Tom looked down at Najki, padding calmly along beside them.

'Maybe it did,' he agreed. 'But don't let's worry

about it now. Let's just spend the rest of the day being triumphant. Tomorrow's coming. We'll try to work it all out tomorrow.'

But inside his head he knew already, and he felt very powerful. For, after all, anyone who was allowed to go for walks with a dog that granted wishes could probably become the boss of the world if he wanted to.

· 6 ·

Najki Searches for Tom

There's always something happening, and a dog like me helps to push it all a little further. After all, if life is supposed to be interesting, it needs to be unexpected, and a dog like me can make things even more unexpected than anyone ever expects them to be. That's the fun of it. Of course some unexpected things can be troublesome, but that's part of the adventure

of What-Happens-Next. My pet, Tomasz, had unpacked everything and, in a way, we were well settled into our new house. But then, instead of taking me out for long walks through the park or down to the sea, he began rearranging all his first arrangements. I got bored with all that shuffling and shifting going on around me, so when he wasn't looking I slipped out of the house and trotted off down Prodigy Street, smelling around telegraph poles, and trying to look as much like any old dog as I possibly could. But deep down I was thinking I might drop in on that boy at Number One . . . what was his name? Oh yes! Tom! How could I forget?

(Of course I carried my magical wagger behind me. I always do. It grows out of me, so I can't leave it at home. No one watching me trot by would realise just how powerful I can be. I am so wonderful . . . a very dog of dogs. That's my secret, and I suppose it's got to be a secret –

but at the same time I'd rather like it if everyone bowed or curtseyed as they watched me trotting past. After all, with a wish-wagger like mine, I could probably conquer the world.

· 7 ·

Mother Up a Pine Tree

At the weekends Tom sometimes got up late, and on this particular Saturday he came into the kitchen (wearing his pyjamas) to find his mum was celebrating Saturday morning by doing one of her big clean-up jobs. She kept time with her dusting and sweeping, by grumbling about the mess other people – Tom, that is – had been making. There was a definite rhythm to her complaints.

'I tidy, tidy, *tidy*!' she exclaimed, (banging

the dust pan with the hearth brush rather as if she was beating a drum). 'Does anyone respect the work I do? No way! Boys! Boys just leave stuff lying around. They never pick up after themselves. Look! A pack of cards spread all over the floor! Did you leave them there, Tom?'

Tom knew he had. And he knew she knew.

'Sorry!' he said. 'I forgot.'

'You forget all the time,' grumbled his mum. 'Look at all those papers all over the table. You could easily have put them back in the right drawer, but no! There they are, tangled everywhere. And who's going to have to sort them out and put them away in an orderly pile? Me! And who's going to get blamed tonight, if you can't find the paper you *want* to find. Me! And, as well as that, I've got to do the dusting and vacuuming and all that sort of thing. And the washing! Not that I can hang it out this morning! There's a storm on the way. A wind storm. Wild winds from the north-east moving in on us – or so the weatherman says.'

Tom thought it might annoy her if she turned round and saw he was still in his pyjamas. He shot back to his room, and did not come back again until he was dressed. He even tied the laces of his shoes and brushed his hair.

When he did slide back into the sitting room he

could hear his mum, still in the kitchen, opening the squeaky window to let some fresh air into the house. And still complaining.

'The whole room smells of old bacon,' she said crossly. 'I'd like to get outside and enjoy the day before that wind comes in on us, and here I am, stuck *inside*, wiping down other people's smears. Look out there! There's that big pine tree, with sparrow nests at the top of it. I wish I was up there in the fresh air, chirping with the sparrows on a morning like this.'

Tom still felt important after the day before. You can't help feeling important if you do a bit of wishing, and your wishes come true. You can't help feeling in charge of life if you happen to have access to the right sort of dog.

'It's hard to climb that tree,' he said (sounding older and wiser than his mum). 'And it's even harder coming down. I reckon if you got stuck up there we'd have to get fire engines to bring you back to earth again.'

His mum did not say anything.

'Anyhow,' Tom went on, using his important voice, 'the sparrows wouldn't be pleased to see you. They're flat-out busy looking after their eggs and babies. They'd be suspicious of you.'

His mum still did not say a word. Tom went into the kitchen, hoping to please her because he had changed out of his pyjamas and tidied himself up. He felt he deserved praise.

The kitchen was empty.

Tom looked left and right. He looked up and down, and then peered around the corner. His mum had disappeared.

The window was open, and a warm, outside

breeze was blowing its way inside, exploring the shelves and the cupboards.

'Strong winds on the way!' Tom called, but no one answered.

'She must have climbed out of the window,' he thought, frowning, and went out by the back door to check the back garden.

There might be storms and strong winds on the way, but right then, in their part of town, it was certainly a fine day. The sun was busy pouring gold all over the garden, and that frolicking breeze was blowing old rose blossoms across the lawn. What with the petals and the daisies, the lawn looked as if snow had fallen all over it, but this was a snow that did not melt away. Wrong season for snow, anyway.

'Mum!' Tom called, and thought he heard a faint reply, but there was no one in sight. What he definitely *did* hear was a sudden bark – and when he looked around he saw that dog from the other end of Prodigy Street, sitting at his feet, smiling and hanging its tongue out as if it was really enjoying the flavour of the wind.

'Hey Najki! Great to see you,' said Tom, bending to give the dog a good, friendly patting. 'You can be useful to me. I've lost my mum. She's just . . . well, she's sort of vanished. So, OK! Walk round the house with me, and see if you can smell her out. Shouldn't be hard. She's been cleaning the fridge so she probably smells of old bacon.'

Najki did as he was told. They walked together around the house, peering under the lemon trees, then into the tool shed. No sign. Tom opened the garage door. There was the car. There was the family bicycle. No Mum! But she *must* be somewhere. Tom decided to walk round the house yet again, just in case they had missed her the first time round. No sign. When Tom came to the kitchen door again his mum was still missing – and not only that, Najki had disappeared as well. He must have got tired of trying to smell out a mum who just wasn't anywhere.

Tom stood wondering what to do next. That busy breeze, blowing round him, growing stronger and stronger all the time, seemed to be filling his ears with echoes of his mum's voice. How could she be *heard*, when she was nowhere to be *seen*? He went inside again, and shouted into every room in the house, just in case she had come back from somewhere, but there was no reply. His mum wasn't making his bed. She wasn't taking an unexpected morning bath. She had completely disappeared.

Tom went outside once more.

'Mum!' he shouted. 'Mum! Where are you?'

Once again he thought he heard her voice, faint and echoing, coming to him from somewhere in the springtime air. Once again he looked *around*. Once again he looked *out*. No sign! Only the shadow of that pine tree, like the head of an arrow, pointing across the back lawn. But then, as he stared down at it, he saw something shifting at the heart of that shadow – another shadow, a smaller, darker one, jiggling inside the wide, grey shadow of the pine tree top. And that shadow-within-a-shadow jogged his memory. His mum had wished . . . had wished for . . .

Oh, you certainly had to be so careful about the things you wished for, just in case whatever you wished might come true.

Tom looked up high into the air at that pine tree, blinking at its lower branches, and then at branches above them, higher and higher still, until he found himself blinking at the very top of the tree where sparrows had built their nests.

And there was his mum. She was sitting on a branch – probably the only tip-top branch that could take her weight. Any branches above that would have been too thin and spindly even for a boy like Tom, let alone a grown-up mum.

Of course! His mum had said she was tired of housework and she had wished to be up in the tree, sitting with the sparrows. Her wish had been granted.

Tom was filled with amazement and admiration for his mum. He had often tried to climb that tree himself, but he had only managed to get halfway up. There was a point where those branches were just too far apart for him to stretch from one to the other, and, though the bark was rough, there was no real toe-hold either. Yet somehow his mum had managed to get right to the top in half a minute less than no time. How could that be? Most mums were not great tree-climbers.

'Hey!' he shouted, and waved to her. She waved back and shouted down to him . . . something he could not quite hear.

'What?' he shouted again, putting his hands behind his ears to show that he was listening. His mum yelled back again, and this time he could make out her distant, echoing words.

'Get me down! Find a long ladder! Call the fire brigade. Get me down.'

Tom took a deep breath.

'How did you get up there?' he called as loudly as he could.

His mum's words came down, faint, frail and far away.

'I don't know! I just don't know.'

'I thought you *wanted* to be there,' shouted Tom – and then he remembered what she had said, as she opened the window to get rid of the old bacon smell. (Of course she had no idea there might be a dog magician waiting under the window. She did not know you should always be careful about what you wished for, because you just might be close to someone who could make wishes come true). Well! There was no doubt about it. Tom must find Najki, and wish his mum down again.

'Hang on a moment,' he yelled as loudly as he could. 'I'll get help.'

As he shouted this he felt as if something invisible came out of nowhere and began pushing wildly against him. Wind. That spring breeze was growing a lot stronger. He stumbled, and heard, from high above him, his mum call out. The top of the pine tree had begun swaying rather wildly, and she sounded very anxious. That wind clouted him again . . . clouds began creeping across the sun, and suddenly he remembered his mum saying that, according to the weather forecast, there was a storm on the way.

'I'll get help!' he screamed again, turning as he yelled and (running as fast as he could), he sped away from the pine tree, past his back door, along the drive and through the gate, bursting, at last, into Prodigy Street.

There was no sign of Najki. The dog must have gone home.

He zoomed down the street, leaping past gates, peering over fences and hedges as he ran. No sign of Najki.

'Whoooooo are you-ou-ou?' wailed the wind

growing stronger and stronger, snatching at him with its invisible net.

Never before had Tom had such a struggle when it came to running down Prodigy Street. But at last he exploded like a boy-bomb into the last house in the street, raced up the steps and beat upon that shining door. All the faces carved into the wood seemed to shift a little, so that they were all staring back at him. It even seemed that one or two of them blinked, surprised by an unexpected visitor.

The door opened.

'Ah, my dear neighbour-from-up-the-road!' said Mr Mirabilis. He was wearing his black cloak with the crimson lining, and looked like a man talking politely from the middle of a smouldering fire.

'I need help,' cried Tom. 'My mum needs help. We need Najki!'

'To tell you the truth,' said Mr Mirabilis, 'he isn't at home. I thought he must be visiting you.'

'He did visit us,' said Tom, 'and he granted my mum's wish. She wished she was up in the top of a pine tree, and that's where she is right now. I want to wish her down again.'

'How long ago did this happen?' asked Mr Mirabilis, looking extremely worried.

'I don't know . . . about ten minutes ago,' said Tom.

'It might be too soon to try another wish,' Mr Mirabilis said. 'Najki sometimes uses a lot of energy making wishes come true, and if the first wish is a big one, he needs time to build his energy up again. But let's go and look for him. And you never know – there may be something I can do. Goodness! What a wind! It *has* come up suddenly, hasn't it? Najki loves wind-riding. I expect he's blowing around somewhere.'

'It must be awful to be stuck on the top of a tall pine tree in a wind like this,' Tom cried, as they jogged down Prodigy Street.

Mr Mirabilis called Najki over and over again, but the wind stole the words as they came out of his mouth and whisked them back over his shoulder and high into the hills. There was certainly no sign of any dogs, though that wind, circling wildly around them, kept howling a hound-howl of its own. Letter boxes clicked and rattled, snapping their teeth at passers-by. That wind caught Tom halfway through a step, and he thought he was going to go whirling up into the pine tree to sit beside his mum. That black cloak of Mr Mirabilis billowed behind them. Sometimes it looked like a devil's parachute, and sometimes

it looked like a pet thunderstorm that was being taken for a wild walk.

As they staggered into Tom's backyard they could see the top of the pine tree – sparrow nests and all – tossing from side to side in the wind. (Clever sparrows to have made their nests so safe and secure.) As for Tom's mum, she was still holding on to the pine tree branch just above her head, but now she was streaming out in the air like a flag waving from the top of a flag pole. Tom could see she was calling, and probably shrieking, but he couldn't hear her. The wind was snatching up every sound she made and whirling it across town, over the hills and off to sea. Sailors, struggling with the storm, might have been able to hear her voice coming out of nowhere, but Tom could not make out a word.

'How can we rescue her?' he cried. 'We need Najki! Where is he? What's happened to him?'

'Najki will be enjoying this gale,' Mr Mirabilis shouted, staring up into the sky. 'Ah! Look! There he is.' He pointed.

There, high above them, Tom suddenly saw the dog somersaulting in the air.

'He's blowing away!' he cried.

'No! No!' Mr Mirabilis cried back. 'He's riding the wind. I told you. He loves wind-riding.'

As he said this Najki caught on to some down-draught. He came swooping towards them.

'Quickly! Quickly!' shouted Mr Mirabilis, but Tom was shouting too.

'I wish my mum was down here with us! I wish she had left all those sparrow's nests behind her.'

As he yelled this wish, he was only looking at Najki out of the corner of his eye. He was mainly staring up at his mum waving like a flag at the top of the pine tree. He was imagining how frightened she must be, trying hard to hang on to that thin branch while the wind lashed around her. And then, suddenly – suddenly! – she disappeared.

'She's blown away,' he screamed. 'She's gone. Gone! Where is she?'

'Tom!' said a voice behind him. Tom spun round.

There was his mum, back on the ground again, her hair billowing out in a wild cloud. Tom raced over to her and flung his arms around her, clinging to her just in case she blew up into the tree again.

'No more wishing! No more wishing!' he shouted at her.

'Come inside at once,' she said, hugging him back. 'It's too windy for us to be out on a day like this.' She looked at Mr Mirabilis. 'You're our neighbour from down the road, aren't you? You should come inside too. We'll have a cup of tea. I definitely need one myself right now!'

'That sounds lovely!' said Mr Mirabilis. 'But I've got to collect my dog. You go on ahead and make the tea. I'll be with you in a minute.'

Tom was so delighted to have his mum back beside him, safely on the ground once more, and preparing to make cups of tea, that he did not worry too much about Najki still somersaulting high overhead.

'Najki can wish himself down again!' he cried.

'No he can't,' Mr Mirabilis called back. 'He can't grant his own wishes, only the wishes of other people. Just as well, or the whole world would turn into a butcher's shop full of fresh meat and soup bones.'

'Wish him down then,' said Tom. 'I will! I can

shout!' And he shouted, 'Hey Najki! I wish you were down here beside us in the garden.'

Nothing happened. High above them Najki turned another somersault or two.

'I don't think he can hear you,' said Mr Mirabilis. 'And if he's going to grant a wish he needs to hear it. On a day like this the wind blows wishes all over the place. Oh dear! I need a true wizard's wand.'

'There's more ways than one of getting in touch with a dog,' said Tom's mum, peering up at Najki. 'And as it happens, I think I do have a wizard's wand – a *sort* of wizard's wand – well, the sort of wizard's wand that will enchant a dog.'

But Mr Mirabilis and Tim scarcely heard her. Now that Tom's mum was safe on solid ground, they had become anxious about Najki, and they did not notice her turning and battling her way back towards the house, the wind lashing at her, probably trying to take her prisoner once more.

High overhead, Najki spun like a top, chasing his own tail. Then he dived into a grey cloud and completely disappeared.

'Oh dear!' cried Mr Mirabilis. 'If only I could fly like a storm-swallow. I'd shoot into that cloud. I'd find my dog, grab him by the scruff of the neck and haul him back to earth again.

He could get lost up there, no telling which way to go! The wind might whisk him far out to sea.'

'Maybe he just might wish himself back again,' said Tom. 'I mean, after all . . .'

But at that moment something clinked and clanked behind them, and the air smelled utterly wonderful. Tom's mum came hurrying towards them. Her hair still streamed in the wind, but she had put on her rubber gloves, and she was carrying a pot with something steaming in it, something smelling delicious . . . something smelling like fresh soup. She reached into the pot and pulled out a big soup bone.

The wind must have liked the smell of that soup. It whirled around them, wildly dancing, and suddenly that soup smell seemed to be spread out everywhere.

'Oh!' cried Mr Mirabilis, forgetting Najki, just for a moment. 'What a wonderful scent. You must be a tremendous cook, madam.'

'I'm very sound on soup!' said Tom's mum. 'And this is a particularly good soup bone.' She danced (with the wind as a partner), waving the soup bone like a strange wand and singing.

'Soup Bone! Soup Bone!
Send your fine scent
Into the clouds
Where the little dog went.
Tell him it's time
For a bit of a treat,
And bring him back barking
To Prodigy Street.'

'Sound on soup, and song as well!' cried Mr Mirabilis, flinging his arms wide. The wind filled his cloak and lifted him off his feet, but Tom grabbed the end of the cloak, and pulled him back down to earth again. And, as he did this, he heard the sound he'd been longing to hear – the sound of a dog barking greedily – then barking some more. Najki came sliding towards them, swooping down on the back of that wild wind.

'Najki!' shouted Mr Mirabilis. 'Here! Here, you good dog! Down! Down!'

And Najki did just what he was told, riding the wind to where his people stood under that pine tree, which was now hitting the sky with its top as if it was a paintbrush working on some vast picture.

'I wish that storm would stop,' yelled Tom.

And suddenly the world seemed to stand still. Suddenly the howling wind hiccupped . . . hiccupped again . . . then hiccupped its howling into nothing

Silence!

'Oh!' gasped Mr Mirabilis. 'What a wonderful family you are. The right kind of bone just when it was needed! The right kind of wish as well!'

Tom and his mum stood looking around their garden, then up into the pine tree, and then behind them at the washing line.

'I don't think we've lost much,' said Tom, 'those pegs were very good ones.'

But his mum was not thinking about wishing or washing.

'Mr Mirabilis! It's getting on towards dinner time. May I invite you to have dinner with us? Tom and I would love to have you and Najki call in. There's nothing but soup, mind you, but . . .'

'But it's wonderful soup,' Mr Mirabilis said. 'I can tell by the smell. And look how Najki is enjoying that bone! Madam, I accept your invitation. The two ends of Prodigy Street will come together and get to know one another.'

And that's just what they did.

That Fine Bone Reward

Nobody can say I don't do my best for others.
Mind you, they can sometimes be surprised . . .
taken aback . . . even annoyed to find (when they
get what they wished for) that they have wasted
a wish by wishing for something they didn't
really want after all. And sometimes a wish can
come true in the wrong kind of way. However
it is great when you grant a wish and someone

rewards you with a meaty bone. Try it yourself. Of course, there are very few wish-dogs with wands for tails out here in the world. I know I am very special. It's surprising more people don't make a huge fuss of me . . . bow when they see me coming . . . give me goodies of one sort or another. Bones are great. I love bones! But people could offer me sausages as well . . . or fresh steak . . . delicate mutton chops . . .

Naturally, a dog like me can't help knowing just how amazingly special he is. I mean, some dogs may have tails like ostrich feathers. Some dogs may have tails like little whips. But my tail . . . well, it may be only a short tail, but it's not just a tail. It is that wonder-wand as well, so that makes me a super-dog. That makes me a dog who deserves to be adored. Of course I knew that Tomasz already adored me, and I think the boy Tom was certainly beginning to adore me too. A dog likes to be adored.

By the way, I think the boy Tom was

becoming pretty pleased with himself. I think
he was beginning to be just the tiniest bit
conceited, because he could wish, and (if we
were together), his wishes would come true.
When we set off down the street he . . . well, he
didn't so much walk . . . he strutted, head high,
chest out, stomach in, grinning at the world as
if he knew all its secrets. Perhaps we both felt
the same way – powerful, but secretly powerful.
No one could tell about us. People would think
he was just another ordinary boy with another
ordinary pet dog. No one would be able to tell
that I was a super-dog taking a pet boy for a
walk. That was the joke we were having with
the world, strolling past strangers in the street . . .
frolicking past friends . . . and then laughing to
each other all the way home. Mind you, when I
did get home there were times Tomasz frowned
at me rather suspiciously, probably feeling that
I was getting too pleased with myself, but of
course I knew better than he did. If anyone

was getting slightly conceited, it wasn't me. If anyone was getting conceited, Tom was the one. Me? Though I am so wonderful, I am as modest as the day is long.

· 9 ·

Unexpected Dog Parties

Dear me!' said Tom's mum. 'The weather forecast this morning said it was going to be a fine day, but there seems to be a great black cloud crisscrossed with flashes of scarlet lightning coming down the road towards us. I'd better race out and bring in the washing.'

Tom ran to the window, climbed cleverly on his old rocking horse and stood up on it, swaying slightly as he looked sideways down Prodigy Street.

'Mum!' he shouted. 'That's not a storm. That's Mr Mirabilis in his black cloak. He's racing down Prodigy Street and – oh Mum, he's coming in at *our* gate.'

Tom's mum was already at the door. Tom leaped from the rocking horse and ran to join her, just as a great knocking began. Tom's mum opened the door politely – very politely and carefully, seeing how that door was being thumped upon. Sure enough, there was Mr Mirabilis, his black cloak twisting wildly around him, as if it was trying to hide him from the world.

'Mr Mirabilis!' said Tom's mum. 'How nice to see you. How about another cup of tea?'

'I'd love a cup of tea,' said Mr Mirabilis, panting slightly, 'but right now I'm rather distracted.' He looked at Tom's mum. 'What's the date today? Twenty-second of March, isn't it?'

'Yes! I think it is,' said Tom's mum.

Mr Mirabilis looked at Tom. 'It's Najki's birthday,' he cried. 'His birthday! But he's gone missing. He was around the house like a good dog this morning, opening his presents and so on, but now he's completely vanished. Perhaps he thinks you've got a present for him. Has he come to visit you?'

'No sign!' said Tom, looking around himself just in case. (For, after all, who could tell about a dog like Najki? He might have worked out a way of making his own wishes come true, and wished himself into Tom's house, thinking they might have a party).

'I've just been doing a bit of outside sweeping,

and I haven't seen him anywhere,' said Tom's mum.

'I'd better find him quickly,' said Mr Mirabilis in a troubled voice. 'I thought he might be riding the wind again (which he does sometimes, as you know, particularly on birthdays), but now I think perhaps he has gone exploring. And there's a man who lives a few streets away who hates dogs. His name is Doctor Felix, and he's a famous Cat Doctor. Rich people from around the world bring their sick cats to Doctor Felix. Anyhow, birthday or not, a dog like Najki could really irritate a Cat Doctor, because, goodness knows, Najki sometimes teases cats in the way dogs do. And of course he can cause a lot of trouble to people who are careless wishers. So sorry for bothering you. I just thought . . .'

'I know about Doctor Felix,' Tom cried. 'Everyone knows he hates dogs. He's put up notices forbidding dogs to come near his house. I'll come and help you search for Najki, because

I'm the one who can recognise Najki, and also I can un-wish things if anyone out there has wished for anything silly. I've had a bit of practice by now.'

'I'll be glad to have your help,' said Mr Mirabilis. 'If a man who hates dogs sees a dog on his lawn – well, you just can't tell what wishes he might wish!'

'I know all about that,' said Tom's mum, remembering what it had been like flapping like a flag from the top of a pine tree, and all because of some careless wishing. 'Off you go, Tom. But don't be late back. You've got homework to do.'

'If I find Najki I'll wish my homework is done,' muttered Tom, setting off beside Mr Mirabilis. 'I'll wish it is done with all the correct answers.'

Tom and Mr Mirabilis came through Tom's gate into Prodigy Street

They looked left and right. They could hear the usual yowling of Miaouler the Yowler two houses down at Number Five, but apart from this, Prodigy Street was quiet and completely empty.

'I'll go left and you go right,' Mr Mirabilis suggested. And that is what they did.

Going right meant that Tom was only in Prodigy Street for about five minutes before it branched out into a main road, a main road whizzing with cars and bumbling with buses. Almost immediately Tom knew Najki had been that way before him. It was a sunny day, but there, on the corner of that busy main road and the road opposite Prodigy Street, a small, dark cloud hovered over a house with a green roof, and rain was showering down on its lawn and garden – very strange when the weather was so fine everywhere around it.

Tom waited for a gap in the line of busy cars, then raced across the road. The owner of that green-roof house was out on the lawn, dancing with happiness.

'I wanted it to rain,' she cried, when she saw Tom looking over the hedge. 'My garden was

so dry, and my hose is leaking. I just stood here wishing for rain to water the tomatoes, and suddenly – look! – it's actually *raining*. I'm so grateful and my tomatoes are just delighted.'

Tom grinned and nodded over the hedge. So far so good! But which way to go now? Then, off to his left, he heard a great howling as if a pack of wolves was chasing prey. Following that

howling noise he turned right again and went
down a narrow street, Windfall Street, that led (he
knew) past a big children's playground. Within
a minute he was staring into that playground,
and there he saw a pack of wild wolves not only
howling but herding a lot of little children into

107

a corner, while their mothers screamed, trying to snatch their children up – trying to make sure their children were well out of harm's way. Mind you, those wolves, though they were howling and herding, did not seem particularly ferocious. In between their howling, some of them seemed to be laughing and wagging their tongues.

'I called my girl over and over again,' one mother was crying to the mother next to her. 'But she wouldn't come. No way!'

'I just wished wildly for a wolf pack to herd my boy home again,' the other mother cried. 'And now look what's happened. My wish has come true. Wolves everywhere! And my boy still won't get off the swings.'

Tom looked over at the boy on the swings and saw a wolf jump at him. But the swing hit the wolf halfway and bowled him over. The boy laughed cheerfully, and Tom could have sworn that the wolf laughed as well. In fact when he looked at those wolves he felt certain they were all in a good mood, playing like puppies and, so far at least, not planning to eat anyone, even though some of those little children looked delicious.

'They're safe enough,' thought Tom, and ran on, leaving the playground, which was full of children and wolves and mothers, full of giggling, howling and screaming.

'But it just shows how careful you've got to be when it comes wishing,' Tom muttered as he ran. 'It's lucky for everyone that I'm such a good wisher!' And, even as he ran, he actually puffed his chest out a little bit.

While running and boasting to himself, he kept looking out for any other stray wishes that Najki might have granted, and, as he ran, the houses along the street grew bigger and smarter, and suddenly Tom remembered that this street, Windfall Street, ended with the property of that very rich man, Doctor Felix the Cat Doctor, famous for curing cats of coughs, catalepsy and catarrh.

But Doctor Felix was also famous for his great hatred of dogs. Dogs chased cats, and cats were definitely his favourites. He had even put up notices forbidding dogs to come near his house. And now it seemed Najki had certainly been this way, granting wishes here and there, switching on that tail of his – that tail which was also a wand. How would Najki manage if he met up with Doctor Felix? Suppose Doctor Felix accidentally wished Najki out of existence. And if somebody wished that Najki would disappear, would Najki have to grant that wish? Tom just didn't know.

Now the first Doctor Felix sign was ahead of Tom. He knew what it would say. He had read it on several occasions.

Tom ran wildly on.

But as he came closer and closer to the notice he was able to make out that it was not quite

what he had expected it to be . . . certainly not
what it had been the day before yesterday.

it read. It sounded the same, but now it meant
something totally different. Knowing a dog is
very different from no-ing it. Three telegraph
poles further on was another notice. Tom felt
certain it would say,

That's what it had always said before, but, once
again, he was wrong. Now the notice said,

and an arrow pointed up to the gate of Doctor
Felix's huge house. The gate (which was usually
shut tightly) was wide open.

111

'Those word-changes could be Najki's work!' thought Tom, and rushed boldly through that open gate. Immediately dogs of all shapes and sizes came bounding to meet him, wagging their tails and tongues at him. And there, out in front of the house, hidden from the street by a high hedge, Tom now saw that a great dog party was

laid out on the lawn – rump steaks, dog biscuits, delicious meaty bones. And in the middle of this great dog feast was a pile of pork chops plaited into the shape of a cake, with a big, blue candle standing tall in the middle of it, burning with a cheerful scarlet flame. A birthday cake, a *dog's* birthday cake. No doubt about it.

Those dogs that had raced up to meet Tom
now raced quickly back again, all anxious to
grab up the bits they had been enjoying in case
some other dog got hold of them. And there,
watching them from the veranda, smiling with
his mouth, but frowning in a puzzled way with
his eyebrows, was Doctor Felix himself. He saw
Tom, and beckoned him on through that pack

of happy dogs, up a
few steps and onto
the verandah beside
him.

'What's brought this
on?' he cried. 'I've always hated
dogs until about ten minutes

ago, and now, all
of a sudden, I find I
like them. How can
a man change his
whole dog-attitude in
ten minutes?'

Tom was looking at the
great dog-party, trying to find
Najki. He must be there somewhere.

'Did you *wish* for a dog party?' he asked. 'Did
you wish for anything?'

Doctor Felix frowned.

'Did I wish for anything?' he said in a
pondering voice. 'Well . . . I suppose . . . I suppose
I just *might* have. There was a little dog running
across the lawn. I threw a golf ball at it, but I
missed it, and, yes, I can remember saying 'I wish
I liked dogs. It would make life so much easier.'
And then, suddenly – suddenly! – I found I *did*
like dogs after years of disliking them. I can
remember saying to myself, 'Good heavens! I *do*

like dogs. I wish I was giving a big dog party.' And the next moment that's what I was doing. This dog-feast was laid out on my lawn, and dogs were coming in from all directions.'

'You have to be careful what you wish for,' Tom said, still looking around for Najki. This is what Mr Mirabilis had often told him. Now it seemed strange to find that he was saying it too, just as if it was something he had thought up for himself.

'Too true! Too true! It's useless wishing for impossible things,' said Doctor Felix. 'Suppose I were to say, "I wish for a dog that spits rainbows." But then . . .'

He stopped abruptly. Something like an earthquake was taking place in the middle of his lawn. As they stared, a stone circle slowly pushed its way up through the grass, rising up in the very middle of the dog's party . . . a round pond appeared, filled with clear water, with a stone dog poised on a dark green stone in the very centre of it. That dog had its nose pointed to the sky, and from its open mouth rose a fine spray of water – clear, silvery water shot through with many little rainbows.

'What's going on?' Doctor Felix yelled, clutching his bushy hair, and, as he yelled this, Tom spotted Najki off to one side of all the other dogs, looking over at Doctor Felix and wagging his tail up and down.

'You can always wish it away again,' Tom said quickly, but Doctor Felix was already over his first shock, and was actually beginning to look rather pleased.

'I've always wanted a fountain,' he said. 'And now – lo and behold – I've really and truly got one. And so easily too! What good luck a few dogs can bring. I never realised until now what charming animals they can turn out to be. After this dog party is over I think I'll get a dog or two of my own.'

'Sounds great,' said Tom, 'but I can see *my* dog over there – that one coming towards us – so I think we'd better get home. Mind you, I'd like to call in some time and see what sort of dogs you *do* get . . . if you do get any, that is.'

A few minutes later he and Najki were racing back down Windfall Street, leaving the barking excitement of Doctor Felix's totally changed house behind him.

'It's your birthday,' Tom said. 'So, Happy

Birthday, Najki!' On they went, past other smart (though smaller) houses, past the children's playground which had quietened down by now. There wasn't a wolf in sight! They strolled past that house with the beautifully watered garden, and back into Prodigy Street.

There, coming to meet him from the opposite end of Prodigy Street, was Mr Mirabilis himself, his black cloak billowing behind him. Najki burst out barking and ran towards his master, while Mr Mirabilis threw up his arms and ran towards Najki.

'Clever boy!' he shouted to Thomas. 'You found him. Where was he?'

'He was throwing a dog party for himself in Windfall Street,' Tom said. 'But I think he was pleased to come home again. I think he's tired.'

'It can happen,' said Mr Mirabilis. 'He gets worn out with that up-and-down wagging of his. Thank you so much for finding him. I have a birthday cake for him at home. You should come and have a slice.'

'Not a cake made of pork chops,' said Tom, looking suspiciously at Najki.

'Heavens, no!' cried Mr Mirabilis. 'A cake made with cream and currants and iced with lemon icing. You'll love it. And so will Najki! It's got his name on it.'

It sounded great. So Tom followed Mr Mirabilis, and Najki followed Tom, frisking and whisking with pleasure at being a dog surrounded by birthday parties.

Just a little later, filled with delicious cake, Tom went back down Prodigy Street, thinking Prodigy Street was lucky to have a boy like him living in it – along with a dog like Najki, of course. Though (he couldn't help thinking), a dog that was able to grant wishes was one thing, but what you really needed was a boy who could wish the right wishes at the right time. Head up! Shoulders back! Chest out! Stomach in! Tom pranced up and down in Prodigy Street as if he was delighted with himself . . . delighted not only with himself and his own cleverness, but with the whole, wonderful world all around him. And to tell you the truth, he was highly delighted with both.

· 10 ·

A Bit More Story-Barking

That dog-party was fun. I got on well with all
the dogs who turned up, all surprised to find
themselves suddenly invited to a dog-party,
but all ready to enjoy it of course. We dogs do
enjoy parties, though no other dogs can enjoy
themselves quite as much as I do. After all, I am
probably the best dog there is.

All the same, I couldn't help wishing there

were more dogs in Prodigy Street. I mean
Tomasz is a wonderful master, and that boy
Tom is a lot of fun . . . but there's nothing like
other dogs if you happen to be a dog yourself.
I'd love a lot of other dogs, particularly if they
were all ready to respect my powers. I've often
wished that Tomasz would adopt another dog,
a dog who would admire me and do everything
I told him to, but my wishes don't work if I
wish them for myself. It is a very strange thing
to wag my wagger and grant wishes to people
around me, but it's even stranger to think that
my own wishes don't seem to count. Someone
else has to wish my wishes for me, and not
many people think of wishing true dog-wishes.

· 11 ·

A Yowling Disaster

These mornings Tom found himself waking up, jingling all over with the secret idea that he just might be turning into the King of the World. He would lie in his bed, blinking himself awake, and then begin to puff up with secret pride. After all, he only had to take Najki for a walk, then wish some wish (wishing carefully of course), and that wish would come true. And he also had the feeling, watching the way Najki bounced along beside him, that Najki rather thought that *he*

might be King of the World as
well. Kings together . . .
King Boy! King Dog!

And these days,
when they set out
(Najki trotting ahead),
Tom was not so much
walking as strutting.
Head held high. Nose up. Chest out. Stomach
in. Left right, left right . . . looking around at the
world as if it was in his power. Yes! The entire
world around him might just as well belong to
him, because he could do what he liked with
it. Of course he knew he had to be careful. No
sense in wishing he had . . . that he had . . . oh,
all the money in the world for
example. Well, not until he had
opened a proper bank account.
And even then some bank
manager might notice, and
start asking awkward

questions. So! No wishing for all the money in the world – not quite yet anyway. Maybe next week.

But there were some things he *could* wish for right now, things he would enjoy.

'I wish that we were going to have a roast chicken for dinner,' he muttered, and saw Najki look up at him, wagging his tail. Of course he would not know if this wish had been granted until he got home. Tom turned around and strutted back towards Prodigy Street, Najki trotting beside him. And these days Najki's trotting also seemed to have a bit of a strut to it, as if that dog were particularly pleased with itself. Mr Mirabilis watched them coming towards him with a small frown on his face.

'I hope you've been careful,' he said. 'No careless wishing I mean.'

'I sort of wished for one little thing,' Tom said. 'But nothing happened. Anyhow I won't know about it for sure until I get home.'

Mr Mirabilis shook his head.

'Najki looks so pleased with himself these days,' he said. 'I think he's becoming just a bit *too* pleased with himself. Granting wishes can make a wish-dog feel very high and mighty.'

'He's been a very good dog,' Tom said. 'I'd love to take him for a walk again tomorrow.'

'We'd both be pleased about that,' said Mr Mirabilis. 'It's fun for him to be out and about with you, and it's a great help for me at present. I have such a lot of work to do. But will you have time to take him out again tomorrow?'

'Plenty of time,' said Tom.

'No careless wishing of course!' added Mr Mirabilis quickly. He suddenly sounded anxious and rather stern.

'No way!' said Tom, and he almost meant it.

As he came up to his own back door a little breeze blew towards him, and Tom smelled something delicious . . . so delicious he stood still just breathing it in.

His mum came out, taking a pile of scraps to the compost heap.

'Tom!' she said. 'We're having a real treat for dinner.'

'Roast chicken!' cried Tom.

His mum looked astonished.

'How did you guess?' she asked him.

'I can smell it,' Tom told her. 'It smells wonderful.'

And later on when Tom and his mum ate their chicken dinner it tasted wonderful too.

Anyhow, next day Tom called in on Mr Mirabilis once more, collected Najki once more, and they set off together once more, strolling down Prodigy

Street . . . well, not so much strolling as *strutting* in their new, conceited fashion.

'King of the World,' said Tom to Najki. 'Well, I could be if I wished to be, couldn't I? I know you've got to be careful what you wish for, so I won't wish to be King of the World quite yet. Maybe next week.'

And then, just as he was tumbling these grand thoughts over and over in his held-high head, a dreadful thing happened.

They were going past Number Five, Prodigy Street, the home of Miaouler the Yowler. That prickly holly hedge had not been trimmed for a while and it was leaning out over the footpath, rather as if it wanted to snatch at them as they walked by, but Tom was used to Prodigy Street hedges, and he took no notice of it. If he had looked at it rather more carefully he might have seen that, even though there was no wind, the hedge was moving a little, rippling slightly as if something was shifting along behind those prickly leaves. However, though Tom did not notice this, Najki did. He stopped and stared, ears picked forward.

'Najki! Come on,' Tom called, getting ready to whistle.

And then, suddenly – suddenly! – DISASTER! Part of the hedge seemed to explode outwards. There was a terrible scream. Out leapt Miaouler the Yowler himself – that gigantic tabby tom, all claws and teeth. Dogs often chase cats, but *this* cat was chasing a dog.

Najki tried to jump up into Tom's arms, but Miaouler the Yowler sprang after him. Najki let out an agonised yelp. Miaouler the Yowler had seized him – had sunk his teeth and claws into Najki's *tail*.

'I wish . . . I wish that Miaouler would change into a . . . a butterfly,' yelled Tom, making up a wish quickly.

But nothing happened. Najki

kept on yelping in agony. Miauler the Yowler
kept on biting and clawing.

There was only one person who could help.
Filled with courage Tom swung into action. He

dropped Najki, then seized Miaouler by the back of the neck and hauled him away. The ferocious cat turned on him and struck out with every claw on every paw, but Tom was too quick for him. He tossed Miaouler high in the air, right across the holly hedge and back onto the lawn beyond. Then he grabbed Najki's collar, and together they pelted back down Prodigy Street. Tom looked over his shoulder as they ran, but there was no cat coming after them. What Tom *did* see however, was a trail of spots and smears . . . scarlet spots

and smears. Najki's magical tail was bleeding
. . . bleeding badly.

There was only one thing for it. Tom had to
cross over to the other side of Prodigy Street,
taking poor, whining Najki back to that house
with the pointed red roof and the winking
upstairs window. Once there, he banged on the
door, and all the carved faces twisted around to
peer at him.

'Help!' he cried, and Mr Mirabilis came
rushing out, anxious to see what was happening.

Mr Mirabilis seemed to know just what to
do for that torn and bleeding tail. He hoisted
his dog up onto a kitchen table, and told Tom
to fuss over Najki, while he arranged a bowl of
warm water, some pink ointment and a bandage.
Carefully, carefully, he bathed that poor, sore

tail. Softly, softly, he rubbed ointment into the scratches. And then gently, gently, he bandaged the tail, bandaged it firmly. That bandage was certainly going to stay put. Tom helped Mr Mirabilis, patting Najki, passing the ointment . . . and then he had an idea. He wondered why he had not thought of it before.

'I wish his tail would get better immediately,' he said.

Nothing happened.

'You see,' said Mr Mirabilis, 'it isn't quite as simple as that any more. We can wish all we want to, but now this tail is *injured*, made terribly sore by tooth and claw. And not only that, I have bandaged it very firmly. Najki won't be able to wag our wishes for a quite a while. Dear me, he might never be able to wag in the right way again.'

'But what will he do?' cried Tom, aghast.

'Well, he'll just have to wait and see. I mean, he'll have to wait until his tail heals. And we'll have to wait and see too,' said Mr Mirabilis. 'Mind you, an accident like this might be good for him. I think that, just lately, he's become rather too sure of himself. I seem to have noticed him *strutting* around the house, all nose-in-the-air. Who can tell? It might even be good for him to have to do without his wish-wand for a while.' Mr Mirabilis looked thoughtfully at Tom. 'Of course you may not want to take him for walks, now that his wish-wand isn't working. It might not be exciting enough for you.'

Tom stared at Mr Mirabilis as if he could not believe what he had just heard.

'Of course I'll want to take him for walks,' he cried. 'Whether his tail is a wish-wand, or just a tail, Najki's my friend. My good friend.'

Najki gave a yelp.

'He understood what you just said,' Mr Mirabilis cried. 'He was so pleased to hear you, he went to wag his tail sideways, but of course that wagging hurt him.'

He gave Najki a careful hug.

'It was my fault,' said Tom. 'I'm taller than he is. I should have been looking out over his head for danger. Will . . . will his tail get better?'

'We'll have to wait and see,' said Mr Mirabilis. His voice was cheerful enough, but he was looking rather worried.

· 12 ·

Difficult Days

It is a terrible thing for a dog like me when
he can't wag his wagger anymore. I tried,
of course. There were lots of times when I
just went to wag as I usually wagged – but
immediately I was overwhelmed by agony, and
my wagger just would not wag. Not an up! Not
a down! Only a day or two ago I had pranced
and padded down the street, feeling in charge

of life. Now I felt like an accident on the side of the road . . . a piece of hairy rubbish that people would step on.

Did other dogs, dogs who had never had magic waggers, feel like this? Was I just like an ordinary dog? I didn't know. However, I did know this. My wagger and its power to grant wishes had certainly made me think I must be the most wonderful dog in the world. Now I had to get used to being a different sort of dog, to leading a different sort of life, and that boy Tom had to get used to a different sort of life too. One moment I had been top-dog . . . King of the World. One moment he had been able to wish for anything and I would have granted his wish. We still went on walks together, of course. We still needed one another. But we didn't strut as we had strutted before. We slid along as if we were ashamed of ourselves.

And then something unexpected – ordinary but unexpected – began to happen.

Nothing in this life stands still for more than a moment. We are always moving on.

· 13 ·

The Ordinary Becomes Extraordinary

Over the next few days Tom took Najki for walks just as usual, but everything felt different. There were times when he found himself going to wish for something just as he had wished in the old days. But then he would remember. He would glance down at Najki's bandaged tail, and feel powerless, as if he was a mere boy and no longer King of the World. Everything had changed. Walking with the dog was no longer the great excitement, full of wonderful possibility, it

had been, and Tom felt – well, he felt he was a boy like the boys on the other side of the street. He felt he was nothing.

And as for Najki? Tom was sure that Najki felt the same way that he did. When they went on their walks Najki did not strut. He did not frisk and frolic as he used to do. He sidled along just a little sulkily, not even trying to wag his poor, bandaged wand of a tail.

'We'll never be Kings of the World now,' said

Tom. 'All the same . . . it's still great to go for a walk or two.'

They were pattering down Prodigy Street as he said this (watching the holly hedge at Number Five very suspiciously, in case Miaouler the Yowler might be crouching under the prickly leaves once again). Suddenly Tom heard someone calling out to him . . . Sarah, of course. There she was, yellow ribbons tying her pigtails up, and a wide smile stretching from ear to ear.

'Great day!' shouted Sarah, skipping up to them.

'There are no great days anymore,' mumbled Tom gloomily.

'Of course there are!' said Sarah. 'Look at the sunshine on the footpath . . . and on the grass there.'

'Sunshine's ordinary,' said Tom, still gloomily. Najki tried to wag his tail and then whined because it hurt him.

'It's ordinary and extraordinary at the same

time,' said Sarah. 'There was sunshine yesterday
– I remember yesterday's sunshine – but that
sunshine down there on the footpath is a *different*
sunshine. And smell those roses.'

There were rose bushes and rose trees in
practically every garden in Prodigy Street. Tom
sniffed, and sure enough, the rose scent burst
in on him. It sprang up his nose and somehow
seemed to fill his head. Until Sarah had mentioned
it Tom had not really thought about that scent.
They walked along side by side, looking at those
patterns of sunshine on the footpath ahead of

them and sniffing in the rose scent, and, though the sunshine and rose scent were so everyday and ordinary, Tom suddenly had the strange feeling that this was the very first time he had ever seen that sunshine, seen it properly, or smelled those roses. Somewhere a bird started singing.

'Listen to that,' said Sarah, but Tom was already listening.

'I think it's a thrush,' he said. 'Or a blackbird, maybe. It's pretty amazing, isn't it? If you think about it, that is. I mean, thrushes and blackbirds sing every day, but even when we hear them, we don't often *think* about what we're listening to.'

For some reason this suddenly struck him as strange. Here he was, wandering along with Sarah and Najki, and suddenly ordinary things like sunshine and scent and sound were meaning something different from what they had meant yesterday.

They were passing Number Eleven, Prodigy Street, a house which had a low stone wall

stretching in front of it. The woman who lived in Number Eleven was standing just behind the wall doing a bit of gardening. Tom touched that wall as he went by. The stone felt rough under his fingertips and, for a moment, he paused, looking down at those stones.

'Great stone!' he said aloud. He had walked past this wall many times before, and he knew the stones in it well, but he had never really thought about them before.

'Very old too,' said the gardener, looking over the wall at them. 'I checked it out. It made itself hundreds and hundreds of years ago. It goes back to the Ice Age, this stone.'

'Gosh!' said Tom. 'I didn't think it was as old as that.'

He and Sarah walked on, Najki trotting beside them.

A mysterious thing was happening to Tom. There were no wild wishes in the air. There was no magical tail-wagging going on. But the everyday world was becoming amazing. The sun, the scent, the sound of it all, the ancient Ice Age stone in a Prodigy Street wall . . .

Tom came to a stop, and Sarah stopped too.

The world was magical. Air was all around him, of course, and he was breathing that air. Breathing was a totally ordinary habit. You didn't have to think about it. It just happened. Air climbed up your nose, went deep into your lungs and came out changed. Yes, it was

ordinary, but Tom found himself thinking how
marvellous it was as well. And there was that
sunlight, falling on him and warming him, just

as it always did, falling on him after travelling ninety three million miles at one hundred and eighty-six miles a second . . . very fast.

'Do you ever think about – about *ordinary* things?' he asked Sarah. 'I mean how *strange* they really are.'

'I was just *thinking* about them,' Sarah said, looking at him in surprise. 'I was thinking that a lot of ordinary thing are utterly, totally, *absolutely extraordinary*. But we get so used to them. We never really stop to think about them.'

'When we do, it's like a sort of explosion in our heads, isn't it?' Tom said. 'I mean, suppose a magician waves a wand . . .' (He looked down, and found Najki looking up at him) '. . . or wags a magic tail or something, it's never quite as weird and amazing as that sunlight on that stone wall.'

Najki couldn't wag his tail, of course, but Tom knew that the dog was agreeing with him. And the odd thing was that this exploding feeling that the world was amazing, and that he was part of all that amazement, didn't make him feel as if he was King of the World. All those past moments of strutting, all the day-before-yesterday's feelings of glory, were fading away. Tom was now feeling (and he knew Sarah was feeling the same thing) that he was part of something more astonishing than anything he could ever have wished for. Even if he didn't smell like a rose, he was sharing the air with roses. That sunlight, warming his face, had travelled such a long way – such a long, *long* way – to fall on him and warm him. The stone under his hand had lived through thousands of years to sit, for a while at least, in a wall in Prodigy Street. And who knew what would happen next?

Tom felt he was dissolving *into* that sunshine . . . into that scent and song around him. Yes! Ordinary, everyday things could be just so astonishing if you really thought about them just for a second or two.

There, at the end of Prodigy Street, Tom knew he was a different boy from the boy he had been at the beginning of it.

A little later, when Tom took Najki home to Mr Mirabilis, Mr Mirabilis looked at him inquisitively, and then looked down at Najki.

'You haven't been wishing for anything, have you?' he asked.

'I haven't needed to,' Tom said. 'It's funny! Sometimes that world out there just changes around you, whether you're wishing or not.'

'Too true!' cried Mr Mirabilis. 'The ordinary world is just so *extraordinary*, isn't it? How did you work that out?'

'Just walking!' said Tom. 'No magic! No tail-wagging! Just walking down Prodigy Street in the sunshine.'

· 14 ·

Another Tail

'Hey, Tom!' said Sarah from down the road. 'Guess what?'

'Just tell me,' said Tom. 'I could guess a thousand guesses, and still not guess right.'

'I've got a job,' Sarah told him. 'I'm looking after a dog for a week. She's a funny sort of dog – a cavoodle - which means she's part cavalier spaniel and part poodle. But, even if she is a bit mixed-up, she's a kind-hearted dog. So if you borrow that dog from Mr Mirabilis we can both go for dog-walks in Paddywack Park.'

'OK – but no wishing for anything,' Tom said. 'Najki's tail is all bandaged up. I can't wish and he can't wag. But even though he can't wag, he'll need to walk, so I'll just go and get him.'

Out at the back of Mr Mirabilis's house was a particularly grand glasshouse, more of a glass palace really, and Mr Mirabilis was busy planting it up with lettuces and tomatoes.

'I'm very happy to let you take Najki out for walks,' he told Tom. 'I know Najki loves exercise, and it's good for me too. But I'm gardening – that's my exercise for today – so I can't take him out and about. It is so lucky that Najki is really fond of you. And I know he likes the company of other dogs. Oh, by the way, I'll be having a gardening day every day this week, so if you could take Najki out every afternoon for a week I'd be most grateful.'

The dog Sarah was dog-sitting was a cream-coloured dog with ruffled-up, half-curly hair. When she hung her tongue out at the world, as dogs do, she seemed to be smiling. Her name was Honeypot. Luckily she got on very well with Najki so, during that week, the after-school walks with Sarah and Honeypot were great fun. They would set off down Prodigy Street, turn into Squodge Lane, then quickly cross over Ominous Avenue. If the Cat-Kicker gang saw them they shouted at them, but they always left them alone. They did not know that, for a while at any rate, Najki wasn't quite the wish-dog that he had been. After that, Sarah and Tom, along with their dogs, would jog down Paddywack Drive and into the Park.

It was like arriving in another land. Once they had that park all around them, they could run around and shout, and the two dogs ran with them, barking brightly at the trees, at the unexpected paths that unwound this way and that, and barking up at the sky too. Then they

would all walk home, rather out of breath what with all that running and shouting and barking. Sarah and Honeypot went in at their gate and Tom would walk down to the end of Prodigy Street, taking Najki home to Mr Mirabilis. Mr Mirabilis and Najki were always delighted to

see each other. And Tom was always sorry to be saying goodbye to Najki. It didn't matter that Najki wasn't able to grant wishes anymore. It was just that having a dog for a friend was wonderful fun.

'I wish I had a full-time dog,' Tom said to his mum. 'Please! Just one!'

His mum gave a deep sigh.

'No way!' she said. 'Don't even think about it. You can borrow that dog from down the road, but we're not having a dog in here. Life is already complicated enough. I do wish you'd forget about dogs for a while. Hey! What's the matter? Did you hear something funny?' For Tom was looking around him quickly, even though he knew Najki wasn't there, and that his mum was able to wish for things without any danger that her wishes might come true. And, after all, if he *had* found himself with a dog of his own, his mum might have blown her top, and no one wants to be around when a mum's top is being blown. Of course his mum had just wished he would forget about dogs. Thank goodness *her* wish had not come true. And anyhow, these days, Tom felt altered in that mysterious way. It was as if all his wishes had somehow melted out into the world around him, and he was living with them every second of the day.

Still, it was great to be able to take Najki (bandaged tail and all) out with Sarah and Honeypot, and it was sad when Honeypot had to go back to her own home two streets away in Squodge Lane, so that Najki became the only dog in Prodigy Street once more. Of course Sarah still had her cat, Mouser, but cats can be very contrary. They will sometimes follow their owners when

their owners go for a bit of a wander, but they don't much like going for real walks, or having adventures in quite the way that dogs do.

And, about this time, Najki became reluctant to leave Mr Mirabilis. He would start out with Tom, and then change his mind and race off home again, just as if he was worried that Mr Mirabilis might have run off without him.

'He has times like this,' Mr Mirabilis told Tom, leaning against his own iron gate, and looking up and down Prodigy Street. 'East, west! Home's best! That's often his motto. Mind you, I don't know for sure, but I think that these days he sometimes visits another dog on his way home.'

'I wish . . .' Tom began.

'Careful what you wish for,' cried Mr Mirabilis flinging up his hands and, quickly interrupting him.

Tom clapped both hands across his mouth. After a moment he took his hands away and said, 'I wasn't going to wish for anything terrible.'

'But you've still got to be very careful,' said Mr Mirabilis. 'Sometimes dogs understand things differently from the way we do.' He paused. 'And now – alas – there's something I've got to tell you. You may not like it, but there's no getting away from it. And it may explain why Najki has become uneasy.'

Tom looked at him nervously.

'I've only just got the house and garden tidied up, and now I find I have to sell up and get out,' said Mr Mirabilis. 'It isn't my fault, and it isn't the fault of anyone in Prodigy Street. It is just that my sister, Sharbalis Mirabilis, is having a great struggle at present. She has seventeen children, all ages, and their father has run away and joined a space programme. He is in a rocket ship right now, on the way to the planet Saturn – that planet with the rings around it. You probably know what a long way off that is. The rocket ship travels very quickly but he won't be home for years. Those seventeen children need a man in the house, not to mention a dog as well. Najki and I have to be off and away.'

'I'm the man in *our* house,' Tom cried.

'No doubt,' said Mr Mirabilis, 'but you see, all my sister's children are *girls*. The oldest girls could *almost* be men of the house of course, but they still need the deep wisdom and good example of a wise uncle. So I have offered to move to their part of the world, and, of course, I must take Najki with me. He will hate saying goodbye to you . . . just hate it . . . you have been so special to him. But there is no way out of it. And don't, whatever you do, wish for things to be different. Wishes like that can cause a lot of trouble. My sister's daughters might melt away like ice creams in the sun. Or perhaps they would find themselves here in Prodigy Street, which is really too small a street when it comes to a family of that size.'

'I don't want you and Najki to go,' cried Tom, but Mr Mirabilis shook his head.

'I *am* going,' he said firmly. 'I'm going because I *must*. As for you, you got on very well before Najki and I came here. Anyhow, I have sold this house to a man who is a very keen gardener. And he does have a dog too, but not the sort of dog to make life complicated. This man will keep the house and garden looking beautiful, but he'll do it by hard work, not dog-magic.'

'It isn't Najki's *magic* anymore,' said Tom. 'Just ordinary life can be magic enough if you think about it. It's just that I really *like* Najki.'

Mr Mirabilis looked at him and smiled.

'So you *know*. You've moved into the mystery of ordinary things around you,' he said. He waved his arms at Prodigy Street. 'It's all out there, isn't it? And you and me, we're not only *in* it, we're *part* of it

161

all . . . the world flows into us, and we flow back into the world. Najki's part of it too. Anyhow, the man who's moving in to my house has a dog of his own. Who knows? He might let you take *his* dog for a walk every now and then.'

'When are you going?' asked Tom in a small voice.

'Tonight!' said Mr Mirabilis. 'And the new owner (along with that dog of his) will move in the day after tomorrow. You'll like his dog. Her name is Honeypot.'

'Honeypot! I know Honeypot!' cried Tom. 'Sarah dog-sat her for a while.'

'Then you certainly won't be completely dogless,' said Mr Mirabilis. 'Good! Prodigy Street is so full of cats it certainly needs a dog or two to even things up.'

He and Tom hugged one another. Then Tom set off, making for his end of Prodigy Street while Mr Mirabilis went back into his house – the house that, after tonight, would belong to someone else, an ordinary gardening man with an ordinary curly, cream-coloured dog.

And, spookily enough, when he woke up next morning Tom could immediately feel that Prodigy Street had changed in some mysterious way. He couldn't say why . . . the very air around him just felt different. After he was dressed, he ran to the gate and looked down the road. And already there was that big van outside that red-roofed house at the end. Once again he could see men carrying boxes and furniture in under the trees. Once again that top window winked at him. And Tom could see Sarah, too, halfway down the street watching that van as well. He jogged down the street to talk to her, but before he could say anything she began talking to him.

'The Scroggins are moving in there. And they're bringing Honeypot with them. Remember Honeypot? I used to dog-sit her.'

'Great!' Tom said. Sarah was so enthusiastic – and, after all, Honeypot was better than nothing.

'And guess what?' Sarah went on. 'Honeypot
has had six puppies. Come and see them.'

Tom was only too willing, and, although they
were moving in, the Scroggins family were only
too willing to take a break, and show them
Honeypot, lying in a dog basket with six tiny
pups – all blind and sprawling and all anxious to
drink milk from a mum who seemed enormously
proud of her pups and wonderfully happy to
have them nestling up to her.

'Prodigy Street is going to be suddenly full of
dogs,' Tom said. 'The cats had better watch out.'

'Except for Mouser,' cried Sarah. 'He'll like
these puppies when they get out and about.'

Tom hoped this was true. Mouser was the sort of cat who could be hard on a dog he did not like. And of course there was always Miaouler the Yowler at Number Five. (Mind you, Miaouler the Yowler had been very quiet just lately.)

'We've got homes for four of them,' said Mr Scroggins. 'When they get a bit older that is. Not *that* one though! And not *that* one. Not yet!'

He was now pointing at the pup at the end of the line and Tom stared at it in astonishment. The more he stared the more certain of something he became. Back when Najki had been a new pup he must have looked exactly like that puppy at the end of Honeypot's pup-row. Najki must be the *father* of this family. He might have been whisked away by his master, Mr Mirabilis, but Prodigy Street would have plenty of reason to remember him as the pups grew older.

The Scroggins did not mind those pups having visitors, so Tom and Sarah visited them every day, watching them as their eyes opened and as they learned how to climb out of their box, and how to play with one another. They grew from little, blind wrigglers, into true puppies.

'Mum says I can have one of the puppies,' Sarah told Tom. 'I'm having the one that looks like a map of the world – that white one with black patches.'

'But we still haven't got a home for *that* one,' said Mrs Scroggins, pointing to the one that looked so like Najki, and Tom suddenly had an idea. If his mum actually saw the pup her heart might soften. She might be enchanted in the same way that he was.

'It might work,' he thought to himself. 'I'll try.'

'I know someone who might like a puppy,' he said to Mr Scroggins. 'Can I borrow that one for ten minutes?'

'Borrow away!' said Mr Scroggins cheerfully. 'Bring him back safely, though.'

Tom lifted up the puppy (which immediately licked him under the chin as if it were absolutely

delighted to be with him), and he carried that pup all the way down Prodigy Street, then turned in at his own gate.

'What have you got there?' asked his mum, and Tom held the puppy out in front of him. His mum looked amazed.

'A pup! An actual pup!' she cried. She looked at it frowning. 'Well, I must admit it is a dear little animal,' she said, rather unwillingly.

'This is the puppy I want to have,' he told her. 'Oh Mum, I do wish I could have this puppy.'

His mum's whole expression altered. It softened. It grew excited.

'Oh, of course you can!' she cried. 'I've always wanted a dog. Oh Tom – having a puppy will make us even more of a family. How exciting!'

Tom was astounded. He stood there with his mouth hanging open. Of course he had hoped his mum would give in and let him have a dog, but he had expected a lot of argument. He had certainly not expected her to agree straight away, and with such enthusiasm. Then he looked down at the pup. It was wagging its stumpy tail but not sideways. *It was wagging its tail up and down.*

Though it was such a new puppy, it was actually granting his wish

'I think – I think it *will* be exciting,' Tom said at last. 'I'll take him home to *his* mother, just to go on with. And in the meantime Mum – Mum, are you listening – we'll practice being careful . . . very careful . . . hugely, *amazingly* careful about what we wish for when our new dog's around.'

the orion star

★ ★ ★

CALLING ALL GROWN-UPS!
Sign up for **the orion star** newsletter to
hear about your favourite authors and exclusive
competitions, plus details of how children
can join our 'Story Stars' review panel.

Sign up at:

www.orionbooks.co.uk/orionstar

Follow us 🐦 @the_orionstar
Find us 📘 facebook.com/TheOrionStar